I'm a Great Big
TOW TRUCK!

by Michael Anthony Steele
Illustrated by Tom La Padula Studio

SCHOLASTIC INC.

New York   Toronto   London   Auckland   Sydney

Mexico City   New Delhi   Hong Kong   Buenos Aires

ISBN 0-439-43434-3

10 9 8 7 6 5 4 3 2 1   03 04 05 06

Printed in the U.S.A.
First printing, January 2003

I'm a great big tow truck!

I like to help people.

I have great big wheels . . .

I have a great
big hook.

I hook it to other cars.

Then I pull them out of the mud and snow.

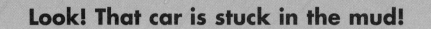

Look! That car is stuck in the mud!

I'll fasten my great big hook to his car and pull it out.

Uh-oh! That lady's car has broken down.

I'll haul her car to the auto shop.

Then it can be fixed.

"Thank you!" says the lady.

Now here are some other cars and trucks that like to help people!

There's a fire truck, an ambulance, and a police car.
They have flashing lights — just like me!

Look — it's an accident.
Maybe I can help!

The fire truck, the ambulance,
and the police car drive away.

But there's still a job for me!

I'm a great big tow truck!

And I like to help people!